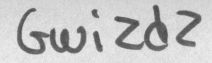

Adapted by Alice Alfonsi

Based on the television series, "That's So Raven", created by Michael Poryes and Susan Sherman

Part One is based on the episode written by Beth Seriff & Geoff Tarson

Part Two is based on the episode written by Dennis Rinsler

New York

Printed in the United States of America

First Edition
1 3 5 7 9 10 8 6 4 2

Library of Congress Control Number: 2005904909

ISBN 0-7868-3836-1

For more Disney Press fun, visit www.disneybooks.com
Visit DisneyChannel.com

Part One

Chapter One

"It's on!" called Raven's father from the living room.

"It's on!" echoed Raven's brother from the staircase.

In her attic bedroom, Raven Baxter heard her family's shouts and nearly dropped her cell phone. "Got to go," she told her best friend, Chelsea Daniels. "It's on!"

Seconds later, Raven was flying down the stairs and running into the living room. Mrs. Baxter came rushing in from the kitchen, and together the whole family crowded onto the living room sofa.

Undercover Superstar was about to start!

As far as Raven and her family were

concerned, *Undercover Superstar* was the most slammin' television show on prime time. Not only did the Baxters never miss an episode, they knew every word of its theme song by heart.

"'From the East Coast to the West,'" the family sang along with the TV, "'we're lookin', we're lookin' . . . we're lookin' for the best . . . we're lookin', we're lookin' . . .'"

"Can you sing?" chirped the show's performers.

"Yeah!" cried Raven, leaping up from the couch.

"Can you dance?" sang the show's announcer.

"Yeah!" cried Raven's brother, Cory, gettin' jiggy with it.

"Lookin' for that one big chance?" asked the TV.

"Yeah, yeah, yeah, yeah . . ." cried Mr. and Mrs. Baxter, bustin' some moves of their own.

"Undercover Superstar, *we will find you wherever you are*," promised the TV. "Undercover Superstar . . ."

"'Oh, yeah, yeah,'" Raven sang along.

When the show's dancers threw off their trench coats and sunglasses to reveal flashy stage costumes, Raven landed on one knee. She threw out her hands and started vocalizing the last *yeahs* of the theme song like a pop diva belting out an encore.

"'Yee-aay, yee-aaaay, yee-aayyy-ee-aiiii-aah-ee-aiiiy!'" she crooned.

In the dead silence that followed, Raven noticed her entire family frowning down at her.

Excuse *you*, she thought as she rose and brushed off her studded jeans. Haven't you ever seen a superdiva take the spotlight before?

"Hi, and welcome to *Undercover Superstar*," the beautiful television hostess announced, "the show where we go to your school, under-cover, to find America's next superstar. Now, if you're out there, we'll find you."

The music began to play again, and the show cut to a commercial. As the Baxters settled back against the couch cushions, Raven crossed her legs and sighed. "Ooh, it would be so cool to be a pop star."

Mrs. Baxter grinned and slapped her daughter's knee. "You know what, honey," she said, "back in the day, your father and I came pretty close."

"Tanya!" said Mr. Baxter, grabbing his wife's arm. "Not in front of the children."

"C'mon, Victor," said Raven's mother, pulling her arm loose. "I think they're old enough to know about Toast and Jelly."

"Uh-oh." Raven cringed, already guessing what was coming next. "I think the question is, do we *want* to know about Toast and Jelly?"

"Your father was Toast," explained Mrs. Baxter, "and I was Jelly."

Oh snap, thought Raven, another trip down memory lane. Otherwise known as Sad and Sorry Avenue.

"We were on a show called *Soul Search*," Raven's mother continued excitedly. "I think we have a tape somewhere—"

"*No, we don't,*" Mr. Baxter said firmly.

Cory's ears perked up. He could actually hear the stress in his father's voice. That could only mean one thing: P.P.E., Potential Parental Embarrassment. *Now* I'm interested, he thought.

"I've got to see that tape," Cory told his father.

"*No, you don't,*" Mr. Baxter repeated.

"Hey, we're back!" exclaimed the pretty announcer on the *Undercover Superstar* TV show. "So let's meet the superstars our undercover talent scouts discovered at schools just like yours. . . ."

Raven's family stared at the TV screen, eager to see what was up with this week's contestants. Raven found herself staring at the screen, too, but she wasn't watching the show any longer.

A familiar tingling had begun racing through her body. And, suddenly, she was watching another sort of show—one that hadn't happened yet!

Through her eye
The vision runs
Flash of future
Here it comes—

Hey, where did my favorite TV show go!? Oh! I'm in a vision. Well, all right, come on then, make it quick. My show's already back from commercial! . . .

So where am I, anyway? Looks like I'm in school . . . and there's the big trophy case near the west entrance. But there's nobody in the hallways. Oh, I know why. The clock on the wall's reading 9:12, so most of the school's in first period already.

Now I'm seeing a skinny blond dude with little round glasses. Looks like he's zipping up a pair of blue janitor's overalls with one hand. The other is holding a cell phone.

"Okay," he's saying into the phone. "I'm in Bayside. I'm undercover and I'm going to find them!"

When Raven came out of her vision, she knew exactly what she'd seen. Obviously, Bayside was going to be the next scouting ground for the *Undercover Superstar* TV show!

"Honey," asked Mrs. Baxter with concern, "did you have a vision?"

Did I have a vision? Raven thought, ready to burst. "Yes, Mom!" she cried, leaping up from the couch. "And he's out there. And I'm going to find him."

Raven was so excited she leaped to her feet and spun like she was the hottest pop-singing diva queen in all of San Francisco. And she was going to be, too! All she had to do was audition for that janitor in disguise. Then the world would finally meet Raven Baxter . . .

"Superstar!"

Chapter Two

"**R**ae, Rae, Rae!" cried Chelsea Daniels the next morning. She had just come through Bayside's west entrance. When she saw Raven, she rushed up to her best friend. "Did you see *Superstar* last night?"

"Yes!" squealed Raven, jumping up and down with her.

Across the hall, Eddie Thomas smiled when he saw his two best friends losing touch with gravity. He wasn't surprised. *Undercover Superstar* had that effect on people. It was the number one show on television. Since it had started running the year before, at least six unknowns had landed recording contracts after appearing on the show.

"*Actually*," Raven confided with a mysterious smile. "I saw *more* than that." She waved Chelsea and Eddie into a huddle. "I had a vision that the talent scout is coming to *our* school," she whispered.

Eddie's jaw dropped. He knew he was the absolute best rapper in the entire school—if not the entire city. One of his secret dreams was getting the chance to audition for someone who could make it happen for him. He could hardly believe what Raven was saying. His secret dream was about to come true!

"Oh, that is big!" he cried, his brown eyes wide. "That is . . ."

For a second, Eddie was speechless. Then he smiled at Raven and Chelsea, spun in place, and broke into the *Undercover Superstar* theme song. " 'From the East Coast to the West, we're lookin', we're lookin' . . .' "

" 'We're lookin' for the best,' " Raven and

Chelsea joined in. "'We're lookin', we're lookin' . . .'"

"'Can you sing?'" crooned Eddie.

"'Yeah!'" cried Raven and Chelsea, bustin' moves down the hallway.

"'Can you dance?'" boomed Eddie.

"'Yeah!'" answered Raven and Chelsea, kicking and sliding like backup dancers.

"'Lookin' for that one big chance?'" the three harmonized together. "'Yeah, yeah, yeah, yeah . . . Undercover Superstar, we will find you wherever you are. Undercover Superstar!'"

As Raven, Eddie, and Chelsea finished their song, a pretty girl with flawless cocoa skin and a pleated skirt and blazer put her hand on her hip and frowned at them.

"Oh," she said, flipping back her long, dark hair. "You guys are *singing*. I thought it was a catfight."

Raven narrowed her eyes at the prissy girl. It

was Jasmine, Bayside's resident "theater queen." As far as Raven could tell, she was also the school's nastiest witch. Well, bring it on, Jasmine, Raven thought. You're not all that, and there's no way I'm buggin' over your sorry little put-downs.

"Ooh, *whatever*, Jasmine," Raven told the girl. "You're not the only one in this school who can sing."

"No." Jasmine lifted her chin. "I'm just the best."

"You think so?" Raven challenged.

"Let's review," snapped Jasmine with a smug smile. "Now, *who* got the lead in the school musical?"

Raven's fists clenched. "You."

"And who's playing 'girl with bucket'?" Jasmine taunted.

"Me," Raven grunted.

Eddie stepped between them. "That just

means you're better at kissing up, Jazz-min."

Jasmine just shrugged. "So, I'm pretty much *better* at *everything*."

Raven rolled her eyes and wondered how the cast of the school musical was going to get through a dance number with Jasmine's *head* taking up most of center stage!

As Eddie shook his own head in disgust, Chelsea's pale cheeks flamed with fury. "You know what," she told Jasmine, stabbing a finger at the air in front of the girl's face. "I would like to see you hold that bucket, Lil' Miss. Yeah. Like to see *that*!"

"Chels, bring it back," Raven said, pulling her crazed friend's finger away from the theater queen's face. It's great that my friends have got my back, she thought, but I don't want Chelsea putting anyone's eye out! "Bring it back, girlfriend. I got it."

B-r-r-r-r-r-i-i-i-i-i-n-n-n-n-n-n-g!

As the first-period bell sounded, Jasmine turned to go. "See you at rehearsal," she called to Raven, "*bucket girl.*"

That does it, thought Raven, stomping after the witch. "Hey, hey! It is girl *with* bucket!" shouted Raven, rolling up her sleeve and making her bicep bulge. "It takes a lot of strength, you know, to carry that bucket. You might want to check it!"

"Rae, Rae, Rae!" Eddie and Chelsea called as they chased her down the hall.

Suddenly, they all pulled up short. A little boy had stepped right in front of them. He was two years younger than Raven and her friends. He wore crisply pressed khaki pants, and a safety-patrol belt across his shoulder.

"Well, well, well, what have we here?" asked the little boy.

"Emmett, the world's most *annoying* hall monitor," Raven replied with attitude. She squinted at the kid's cheap gold badge.

"Hey," Emmett snapped, "I didn't skip two grades to take any lip from the likes of you."

As Emmett waved his pad of yellow *You're busted!* slips, Raven, Eddie, and Chelsea took a step back with dread.

"What are you waiting for?" barked Emmett. "Next time it's detention!"

Raven, Chelsea, and Eddie immediately took off. They rushed past the school's trophy case and around the nearest corner.

With glee, Emmett watched them run. "They fear me," he murmured with satisfaction.

After Raven and her best friends were out of Emmett's line of sight, they stopped, turned, and backtracked. Raven snuck a peek around the corner to make sure Emmett was gone, then she waved to her homies. They followed her back to the west hall again. This was where she'd had her vision, right in front of the trophy case.

"All right, Rae," said Chelsea, "now, this talent scout you saw, what exactly, you know, did he look like?"

"Well, he kind of—" Raven's jaw dropped. Slowly, her arm rose and she pointed across the hall. "He looked just like *him*."

It was just like her vision. The skinny blond dude with the little round glasses was zipping up his pair of blue janitor's overalls with one hand. And with the other, he held the cell phone to his ear.

"Okay, I'm in Bayside," the man said into his phone. "I'm undercover, and I'm gonna find them!"

Chelsea leaned close to Raven and Eddie. "Okay, you guys," she said urgently, "now we need to be on the lookout for a guy who looks just like him."

Raven squeezed her eyes shut. Just when she thought Chelsea was sharpening up, she'd take her whole "*Duh!*" thing to the next level.

"Chels!" Raven barked, hoping to wake the girl up. "That *was* him."

"Oh?" Chelsea scratched her head and looked across the hall again. "Well, that was easy. Ooh, *omigosh*, I totally know just what I'm going to sing for him!"

Eddie's head nodded like a bobble-head doll. "Hey, hey, and I got the perfect rap!"

Raven frantically waved her hands like she was trying to stop a plane from crashing. "No, no, no, guys. We have to chill. Okay? We've got to keep this a *secret*. If someone finds out that that is a talent scout from *Undercover Superstar*, then everyone is going to want to audition."

"Yeah, yeah. Right, right, right," said Eddie. "Good thing the only people that know about this is us. Can I get an *amen*?"

"Amen," chirped Chelsea.

Eddie was in total agreement with Raven on this one. They would have to keep this quiet. Every last student in their school would be discovering their inner divas if they knew an *Undercover Superstar* scout was hanging in their halls.

"Your *momma's* going to want to audition!" Eddie joked. Then he, Chelsea, and Raven headed to their first-period class.

As the three friends strolled along, none of them noticed the girl who'd been lurking in a nearby doorway. It was Jasmine, the theater queen and wannabe superstar. She'd overheard every word.

So, thought Jasmine with a sly smile, the *Undercover Superstar* scout is masquerading as a janitor. Well, thank you very much, Raven Baxter. I guess even a *bucket girl* can be useful now and then.

Chapter Three

Come on, come on, Cory griped to himself later that day. It's *got* to be in here!

He was kneeling in front of an open cabinet in the Baxters' living room. On the shelves inside were dozens of videotapes. Most of them were home movies.

Let's see what we've got, Cory told himself as he read the labels. *Grandpa's Retirement Dinner, Cousin Rondell's Wedding, Cory's First Steps* . . . Aww, how cute! *Raven's Fifth Birthday Party* . . . Ugh, there's one we can record over. *Vegas Vacation, Toast and Jelly* . . .

"*Toast and Jelly* . . . Yes!" he cried.

"No."

Cory turned to find his father standing

behind him. With one quick move, Mr. Baxter's big hand had plucked the Potential Parental Embarrassment from Cory's sticky fingers.

Dang, thought Cory, I've got to do some damage control here. "Dad!" he pleaded, "how bad could it be?"

"Bad enough," said Mr. Baxter, walking toward the front door. "I'm throwing this tape out."

"No, you're not," said Cory's mother, snatching the tape from her husband as she swept in from the kitchen. "Honey, you never throw away your memories, no matter how humiliating. Some day . . . in a hundred years or so . . . you may laugh at this."

Mr. Baxter folded his arms in a huff. "Fine," he replied, taking the videotape back from his wife. "But until then, I'm going to hide this someplace where Mr. Nosy can't find it."

Cory rubbed his little hands together. "Ooh, I love a challenge."

"You do, huh?" said his mother. "Well, when's the last time you practiced the piano?"

Cory grimaced. *Busted,* he thought.

"*Mmm, hmm.* Exactly, get to it," ordered his mom.

"But, it's boring," Cory protested.

"Honey, how would you even know?" Mrs. Baxter countered. "You know, if you actually practiced, maybe someday you could be on *Undercover Superstar.*"

"*Undercover Superstar,*" whispered Cory. As he walked across the living room, to the piano, his mind took another little trip—into fantasyland.

Cory sat down and stared at the eighty-eight keys of ebony and ivory. *Whoa,* he thought, I can almost hear that fly TV lady introducing me on *Undercover Superstar.*

"Let's welcome our next superstar! Now, give it up for the 'king of the keys,' Cory Baxter!"

That's right, thought Cory. I can just see myself walking onto the stage in my flashy suit of black silk, embroidered with solid-gold musical notes. I'd have gold shoes, too. And my sunglasses would be encrusted with diamond bling-bling.

I'd sit down at a grand piano decorated with black-and-white animal print. Two beautiful dancing girls would be wearing black-and-gold costumes and waiting for me to start my music. I'd crack my knuckles, then send my fingers dancing across those eighty-eight keys.

I was once a little punk, Cory began to sing in his head, "*back then, tell me who would've thunk . . . I'd be the king of the keys? . . . The ebony and ivories . . . bring the ladies to their knees . . . I'm the king of the keys. . . .*

Cory's head bobbed to the beat. He could almost hear the audience clapping along.

Mamma said don't hesitate . . . jam down with those eighty-eights . . . now I'm the king of the keys . . . doin' what I please . . . Ho! Make the ladies scream with ease . . . I'm the king of the keys . . . I'm a musical Hercules. I'm the king of the keys . . . baby, I'm the king!

With eyes closed, Cory could see the audience was blown away by his performance. In his mind, he could actually hear the crowd chanting his name. *Cory! Cory! Cory!*

"Cory? Cory?"

Cory suddenly realized the crowd wasn't chanting his name. His mother was! When he opened his eyes, he saw her standing right beside him with her hands on her hips.

"You're supposed to be practicing," Mrs. Baxter reminded him.

Cory shook his head and watched his mother

return to the kitchen. "Practice?" he said, rising from the piano bench.

As far as Cory was concerned, he'd just given the performance of a lifetime. And nobody should have to *practice* after that!

"*Please*," he murmured, heading for his bedroom to play video games. "I'm the king of the keys!"

"Come out, come out, wherever you are," Raven muttered to herself.

"That *Undercover Superstar* scout has got to be around here somewhere. All I have to do is find him."

Between her morning classes, she'd checked out the auditorium, the gymnasium, and the locker rooms. But she'd had no luck. Finally, she spotted him! He was striding down the first-floor hallway, pushing a bucket cart and mop.

"*Meee, meee, meee!*" sang Raven, trying to warm up fast. She blew into her pitch pipe. "*Mee, mee, mee!*"

Her plan was perfect. She would follow the fake janitor into an empty classroom. Then she'd let loose with her musical number "Shine," a song she'd written herself. But Raven's plan was suddenly interrupted—along with her "Mee, mee, mee"-ing.

"Aha!" cried Emmett, the hall monitor, jumping in front of her. He pointed his finger at her pitch pipe. "Singing in the hallway?"

He shook his head, wrote up a yellow slip, and slapped it into her hand. "You'll be spending lunch in detention."

"What!" cried Raven, reading the detention slip. "You little power trippin', grade skippin', wannabe police!"

But Emmett the Detentionator had already walked away to look for his next victim.

Raven shuddered with fury and balled up the slip. Then she took a deep breath and tried to regain her focus.

"Shake it off," she told herself. "Don't let him hurt you, Raven. You're going to be famous. You're going to be a superstar!"

She had lost sight of the *Undercover* scout by now. And she hurried through a crowd of students to find him again. She caught sight of his blue overalls turning the corner at the end of the hallway.

"Well, all right," Raven murmured, rushing forward to catch up. When she saw where the fake janitor was heading with his mop and bucket cart, she knew it was her lucky day.

He's going right into an empty classroom, she realized excitedly. This is perfect. It's just like I planned it. Here I go with my audition! Now it's my turn to "Shine"!

But when Raven rounded the corner and leaped through the classroom door, she realized the room wasn't empty. Jasmine was already there—and dressed for *her* audition.

The girl had obviously raided the drama club's wardrobe closet. She wore a 1950s-style dress with layers of petticoats to make the skirt puffy. She had white gloves on her hands, pearls around her neck, and old-fashioned patent-leather pumps on her feet.

The room's desk chairs had been pushed to the back. And the teacher's desk had been removed from the raised platform at the front of the room.

Someone hit a boom box and 1950s-style bebop music filled the air.

"'Hey, floor mopper,'" Jasmine began to sing as she walked up to the scout in overalls. "'Here's a showstopper. . . .'" She pushed him into a chair at the center of the room. "'I've got the stuff that you're looking for. . . . Listen to me singing. . . . I'm a goddess!'"

"'Bow down, she's a goddess,'" sang her chorus of followers from the drama club. All of them were dressed just like her, like they'd stepped out of a 1950s musical.

"'And I can dance and act . . . and still be modest,'" sang Jasmine.

"'Bow down, she is flawless!'" crooned the chorus. They spun and kicked and danced around their superstar, Jasmine.

"'When it comes to the fine arts, mister, I'm the finest,'" Jasmine sang. "'Around the theater I'm known as Your Highness!'"

Dang, thought Raven, at least the little prissy princess got *that* right!

"'I belong upon that TV screen—'" Jasmine sang.

No way, *uh-unh*! No you *don't*, thought Raven. But to her horror, the *Undercover* scout was bobbing his head in time to the beat of Jasmine's song. It looked like he was actually enjoying it!

"'I'm the theater queen,'" she sang. "'You have found your superstar. . . .'"

"'Theater queen!'" echoed the chorus.

"'Didn't have to look too far . . .'" she sang.

"'Theater queen,'" they echoed.

"'Listen to my perfect voice. . . . Theater queen . . . you don't have any other choice. . . . I'm the greatest thing . . . you've ever seen. . . . I'm the theater queen!'"

As Jasmine finished her number, the talent scout in overalls grinned and applauded wildly. "Amazing! Fantastic! You should be on TV!" he cried.

Raven's heart—and hopes—sank.

The fake janitor left the room with his mop and bucket cart. And Jasmine strutted toward the doorway.

"Thanks for the tip, Raven," she said with a smug smile. "You know, you really should work on that whole 'keepin' it a secret' thing."

"Yeah, actually," Raven muttered in total and complete defeat. "I should really work on that."

Chapter Four

Raven was completely depressed. Her psychic vision had handed her the perfect chance to secretly audition for an *Undercover Superstar* scout. And once again her big mouth had blown it.

At lunch, she ignored Emmett's detention slip and went to the cafeteria with Eddie and Chelsea. She had no choice but to break the bad news to her best friends.

"Jasmine did a full-blown production number for the new janitor," she told them. "And the guy applauded."

Chelsea's face fell. She tried to argue that maybe the new janitor was just being polite. But Raven didn't buy it.

Then Eddie tried to argue that maybe the janitor would think it over and change his mind. "Maybe he'll be keeping an eye out for a better singer."

Raven wanted her best friends to be right, but she assured them that the scout looked really pleased with Jasmine's singing. "He even said she should be on TV!" Raven cried. "What more could seal the deal?"

Later that afternoon, Raven, Eddie, and Chelsea were coming down the school's main staircase when Raven stopped dead. She pointed to show her friends what she'd noticed.

The *Undercover Superstar* scout was standing right beneath them. He was talking on his cell phone again, and it looked like he was trying to keep his conversation a secret.

"No," said the man into his cell phone, "I *haven't* found what I'm looking for yet. But don't worry, I still have this afternoon."

Raven's jaw dropped.

When the fake janitor closed his cell phone and walked away, Eddie turned to Raven. "Man, did you hear that, Rae?" he cried. "He still hasn't found what he's looking for!"

"I know," said Raven. "That means Jasmine didn't get it. We still have a chance to audition!"

"Yeah," Chelsea agreed excitedly. "Okay, you guys, but this time, we've got to be extra, *extra* careful. Nobody can find out that the new janitor is really a talent scout for *Undercover Superstar*!"

Raven squeezed her eyes shut. Chelsea had just announced "the secret" so loud that anyone within ten feet surely would have heard it.

Slowly, Raven turned around. A dozen kids stood on the steps behind her. Their eyes were wide with astonished excitement.

Raven frowned. "You all didn't hear that, did you?" she asked.

The kids all nodded.

"Oh, but you did," Raven realized.

Eddie threw up his hands. "You know what this means?" he told Chelsea. "Every man for himself!"

"Or woman," Chelsea added as the two headed to their next class.

"Give it up, Raven," said a familiar voice.

Raven looked again and saw that Jasmine was standing on the crowded staircase, too. The theater queen pushed through a few kids to tell Raven: "If he didn't like me, there's no way he's gonna go for you, *bucket girl.*"

"Oh, oh!" Raven sputtered as Jasmine flounced off. "It is girl *with* bucket!" she cried angrily. "*W-I-T-H!*"

Then Raven sighed and wondered for a second if what Little Miss Put-down said was true.

No, Raven decided. No way. A girl like

Jasmine, she'll always try to rattle you into doubting yourself, but . . .

"You know what?" Raven called after the theater witch. "I'm *not* giving up. I'm a superstar!"

The rumor about the talent scout took off like a rocket on fire. For the rest of the afternoon, the halls of regular old Bayside looked more like the School for Performing Arts.

Between every class, kids would search the man out and launch into their acts. There were ballerinas doing pirouettes, baton twirlers turning cartwheels, tap dancers kicking their legs, and singing groups breaking into three-part harmonies. There were sax players, jugglers, and hip-hop dancers.

At one point, a surge of kids came at the man like a tidal wave. "'*Undercover Superstar*,'"they sang. "'We will find you wherever you are. . . . *Undercover Superstar* . . . We will find you . . . wherever you are!'"

The new janitor was surrounded—and overwhelmed. He picked up his broom and quivered as the kids closed in.

B-r-r-r-r-r-i-i-i-i-i-n-n-n-n-n-g!

As the late bell sounded, the kids suddenly dispersed. And the new janitor sighed with relief. "Saved by the bell," he muttered as the kids *finally* left him alone.

With the hallway completely empty, the man thought he was going to have some peace and quiet. But he *thought* wrong.

"You know, hallways are such funny things, aren't they?" said a female voice.

The new janitor spun to find Chelsea sitting on the school's main staircase.

"Sometimes, so full of life," she told him as she rose. "And other times . . . so *lonely.*"

"Huh?" murmured the janitor.

Chelsea had gotten a hall pass and changed out of her school clothes. She was now wearing a black leotard with a black tuxedo-style tie and tails.

Here we go again, thought the new janitor when he saw her costume.

Chelsea snapped her fingers and some unseen hand tossed her a top hat. She snapped her fingers again and every light in the hall went out but one. It shined down on her like a stage spotlight.

"'Every day in French class,'" Chelsea sang, placing the top hat over her long, red hair. "'I ask Mademoiselle for the girls'-room pass, and my heart fills with emotion . . . as I'm struck once again by the same old notion. . . .'"

A cane came flying through the air. Chelsea caught it with one white-gloved hand.

"'All alone in the hallways, as always,'" she sang, twirling the cane, "'just the stairwell, the lockers, and me . . . because the hallways, in big ways and small ways . . . is such a lonely place to be. . . .'"

In her high-heeled tap shoes she began strutting down the hallway like a Broadway chorus girl.

"'Yes, alone in the hallways, as always,'" she sang, "'the trash cans are my only friends. . . . I've always hated to be isolated, but then third period ends.'"

From out of the shadows, more chorus girls danced into the spotlight with high-heeled tap shoes. All of them were dressed in black tie and tails, just like Chelsea.

"'Then, these halls I was in,'" sang Chelsea with her dancers behind her, "'will soon be buzzin' . . . with students and teachers . . . and jocks in their sneakers. The bells start ringin', and everybody's singin' . . . I won't be alone . . . on my own . . . in the hallways . . . no-ah mo-o-o-o-o-o-re!'"

The man in the overalls stared at Chelsea in disbelief. "Is *everyone* in this school trying to get into show business?"

Chelsea put a hand on her hip. "Whatever gave you that idea?"

Just then, Raven marched up to the *Undercover* scout. She'd gotten herself a hall pass too. "Hi," she said confidently. "I just need to talk to you for a quick second. I have a *song* that—"

"No!" cried the new janitor, putting up his hands. "No. No. No more!" He shouted, taking off down the hall with his broom.

"No. Wait!" Raven called after him, "I'm not like the others!" *Dang*, she thought, stamping her foot. She turned to Chelsea in total frustration. "But, I saw him first!"

Chelsea shrugged guiltily, and Raven took off down the hall. She chased after the scout, all the way to the school's gymnasium. But when she pulled open the heavy wooden door and ran inside, she couldn't believe her eyes.

Eddie was in there. He'd been practicing on the basketball court with his gym class. But when the scout from *Undercover Superstar* burst into the room, all the practicing had stopped. And the audition began.

"'History in the makin',"' rapped Eddie. "'Believe me you ain't never heard . . . a young man that can blaze the track! . . . Ridiculous cat . . . that can dribble behind his back. . . .'"

Raven watched as Eddie took a point position. His teammates, all dressed like him in their bright yellow Bayside Barracuda T-shirts and shorts, lined up behind him. They dribbled their basketballs in a coordinated rhythm to underscore Eddie's hip-hop beat.

"'It's greatness within my blood,'" rapped Eddie, "'and can't nobody understand it . . .

but when you hear this track . . . I bet that I'm'a see you dancin'.'"

Dang, thought Raven, Eddie is the bomb!

"'Just one shot . . . is all I really need . . . to bring it to yo' ankles . . . and make you wiggle your knees,'" he rapped. "'I'm guaranteed to make the nation wanna follow me. . . . I got the ladies like oohh child, I need to breathe, now . . . watch Eddie as I hold it steady. . . . I'm an undercover superstar . . . but y'all ain't ready. The game is full of gimmicks, so I'm 'bout to make y'all feel me . . . take a piece of me and keep it. . . . May the world get ready. . . . Bounce!'"

Then everyone *did* bounce. Eddie and his team busted a series of incredible hip-hop moves—while dribbling basketballs!

But the audition was over when the gym teacher came barreling through the door. He frowned at his team.

"What the—?" he cried.

With a loud blow of his whistle, he yelled for them to get back to practicing basketball. And the *Undercover* scout left the room with his broom—and Raven hot on his trail.

Meanwhile, back at the Baxter house, Cory hadn't given up his search for Dad's Most Embarrassing Videotape.

He looked in every hiding place he could think of—the kitchen, the den, the closets, even his own bedroom. He looked under the couch and between the cushions. He tried the vases, the fireplace, and the umbrella stand, but he couldn't find it anywhere!

Cory was double-checking the drawers in a living room chest when he heard a deep, suspicious voice boom behind him. "Cory, what are you doing home for lunch?"

Cory gulped and turned to find his father

frowning down at him. *Whoa,* thought Cory, better derail this train fast.

"I missed you, Daddy!" Cory cried in his I'm-so-sweet-and-innocent voice. He stretched out his arms. "Hug!"

But Mr. Baxter knew when he was being punked. "Son, you are wasting your time," he warned. "I hid that tape in the last place you'll look."

Cory huffed. "Fine," he snapped in frustration.

His father left the room and Cory sighed. "You really think I care about that tape?" he muttered, walking over to the piano and dropping onto the bench. "That amazing, serious, forbidden tape!"

Cory sighed again and tried to think like his father. If I were my dad, he thought, where would I hide a humiliating videotape from my son?

Absently, Cory began to plunk on the keys of the piano. *Ting, ting, ting,* went the notes. *Ting, ting, THUD—*

Cory frowned at the piano keys. He hit the bad note again. *Thud, thud, thud!*

Something was wrong with the piano, he realized. He opened the lid, looked inside, and there it was—his parents' *Toast and Jelly* videotape!

Hallelujah! he thought. Then he turned his face to the heavens and grinned. "Thank you," he said.

He could hardly believe it. His father's most embarrassing moment was now in his hands.

Chapter Five

"**L**itterbugs," griped Emmett the hall monitor. "Worst kind of criminals."

The little boy in the safety-patrol belt picked up the stray ball of paper and threw it into the nearest trash can.

Inside the can, Raven held her breath. She didn't know how much time Emmett would give her in detention for impersonating trash, but she certainly didn't want to find out!

When she was sure the coast was clear, she peeked over the top of the can. All right, Mr. *Undercover* scout, she thought, just try to get away from me now!

Sure enough, the new janitor rounded the corner. When he saw the overflowing trash can, he loaded it onto his dolly and carted it into the cafeteria.

Inside the can, Raven gathered her courage. This is it, she told herself. You better pop out before he delivers you to the cafeteria Dumpsters!

"How y'all doin'?" Raven chirped. She popped out of the can, and the fake janitor nearly had a heart attack. He jumped back in surprise, but Raven quickly climbed out. "Look, about that song. I just want to talk about it."

"What is going on around here!" cried the man.

"Well, I just want to sing a little song for you," Raven explained.

"Well, I'm just trying to do my job," the *Undercover* scout replied.

"And I am going to make your job a lot easier," Raven assured him. She was a little self-conscious with everyone in the cafeteria looking on, but she wasn't going to quit now. This is it, she thought, it's my turn to "Shine"!

She snapped her fingers and Chelsea hit the boom box. A funky beat filled the cafeteria.

"'Oooo, ooo, oh, oh,'" she began to sing. "'I-ah-ah . . . know what I'm all about, nobody's gonna change me. And I-ah-ah stand my ground, won't deal with neg-a-tiv-ity.'"

Jasmine threw her a nasty look, but Raven ignored the girl.

"'I got my mind made up,'" Raven sang even louder. "'I'm gonna do whatever makes me happy. One step at a time, I choose my own de-eh-eh-eh-stiny.'"

Some of the dancers from the drama club ran over to join her. They copied her steps and busted some moves to the boom box beat.

"'There's no doubt,'" Raven sang. "'It's about my dreams coming true. Won't stop. Can't stop. Do what I need to do.'"

Raven clapped her hands and spun. She slid and kicked and bounced. The dancers behind her copied every move exactly.

"'I can stand up on my own,'" she sang, leaping onto a cafeteria table. "'My own! No one can bring me down-down. I know I'm gonna shine-shine, shine-shine.'"

The kids all around her in the lunchroom started to clap and dance.

"'I'll never, ever lose sight of what I want in my life,'" Raven sang. "'I'll stay true to myself. . . . No one can tell me what the future holds. I'll stay strong no matter. I will survive. I'm gonna shine!'"

The beat started driving and Raven closed her eyes. She imagined herself on the *Undercover Superstar* studio stage. Her costume would be studded with rhinestones. Dancers would surround her, coordinating their kicks and slides and supersharp dance moves with hers.

"'I can stand up on my own. No one can bring me down-down,'" she sang. "'I know I'm gonna shine-shine, shine-shine. . . . I can hold my head up high. I'm gonna make it through-through. It's my time to shine-shine, shine-shi-i-i-i-ne!'"

When Raven finished, all the kids in the whole cafeteria leaped to their feet and cheered.

"She's my friend!" cried Eddie, rushing up to her with a proud grin. "She's my friend, right here!"

Raven thanked Eddie, but he wasn't the person she was trying to impress. Holding her breath, she turned to find out what the talent scout thought of her song.

"Unbelievable, kid!" he cried, clapping like mad. "That is the *best* performance I've seen all day!"

Raven's eyes widened in shock. She jumped up and down and clapped her own hands. Everyone around her seemed really happy for her—everyone except Jasmine. The witch was shooting nasty eye daggers, but Raven finally had the upper hand.

"Well," she told the theater queen with a grin, "it looks like *someone's* found what he's looking for!"

"Yeah!" agreed Chelsea, snapping her fingers in Jasmine's face. "That's right. That's right."

Jasmine pushed Chelsea's hand away. She turned to the man in the blue overalls. "Okay, so you think *she* belongs on *Undercover Superstar?*"

"Oh, I think you *all* do," said the man.

Eddie, Chelsea, Jasmine, and all the other

student performers whooped with glee. Then the man added, "It's just too bad none of their talent scouts were here to see it."

"Yeah," said Raven, only half-listening. "That's too ba—*What* did you just say?"

All the whooping and hollering suddenly stopped. Dead silence descended on the cafeteria.

"Wait," said Raven, "I thought you were undercover."

"I am," said the man, nodding his head. "For the health department."

A gasp went up all over the room.

Raven still couldn't believe it. "Aren't you looking for talent?"

"No. I'm looking for *bugs*. You know, spiders, ants, cockroaches . . . and I've got to tell you something. This place is crawling with them!"

"Oh, gross!" cried the crowd. Then with

grunts and groans of extreme disappointment, the knot of hopefuls dispersed until Raven found herself standing all alone.

"Excuse me. . . ."

Raven looked up to find one person still there. It was Emmett, the hall monitor, with a big smile on his face.

"That was great," he said.

"Really?" she replied. "Thanks."

Then Emmett's smiling face fell. "No dancing on the tables," he barked as he ripped off a yellow *busted* slip and slapped it into her hand. "See you in detention."

Raven sighed and shook her head. "Thanks," she muttered. "See you there."

A few days later, Raven was still completely depressed about her *Undercover* error. She barely noticed the new janitor mopping the floor near her locker.

She was about to head out the door, when the janitor stepped right in front of her. He wore blue overalls and a blue cap. And he had a fake-looking mustache that was two shades darker than his long, light brown hair.

"Excuse me," said the man with the fake mustache. His voice sounded weird, like it was fake, too. "Are there any kids around here who can sing or dance, or want to be a superstar?

"Sorry," Raven said, stepping around the funny-looking guy. "I'm not singing for no more janitors!"

When Raven was gone, the janitor removed his mustache and cap. Long, brown hair tumbled down. The janitor wasn't a janitor at all. It was the pretty announcer from the *Undercover Superstar* television show!

The woman shook her head and threw down the mop. She just couldn't understand her bad luck. Dozens of Bayside kids had sent e-mails to the show saying their halls were full of talent. But every kid she asked about singing or dancing just waved his or her hand and said the same thing as the girl she had just spoken to.

"Oh, well," said the scout as she headed for the door. "Maybe I'll have better luck at Jefferson High."

That night, Raven was in her attic bedroom when she heard the call again.

"It's on!"

At Cory's shout, everyone in the Baxter house came running. They dived onto the living room couch and stared at the TV. But what they were seeing wasn't their favorite prime-time show.

"Hey, wait a minute," said Mr. Baxter. "*Undercover Superstar* isn't on until tomorrow."

"I know," said Cory with a sly smile. "I've

got a *new* show I think you guys will enjoy."

Cory turned up the volume. A handsome TV announcer cried, "Welcome to *America's Most Embarrassing Parents!*" A theme song played, and the announcer introduced the opening segment. "Our first tape was sent in by Cory B. I guess he was too embarrassed to use his last name."

The studio audience snickered.

"Let's see why," said the announcer.

On the couch, Cory's mother looked at her son. "You didn't."

Mr. Baxter looked at his wife. "He wouldn't."

"This act is called 'Toast and Jelly,'" said the announcer.

"Uh-oh," said Raven. "But he did."

On the Baxters' television screen, the Toast and Jelly act had already started. As disco music began to play, a young couple jumped in front of the camera. Along with grins from ear to ear, the pair wore the kind of clothes that hadn't been in fashion for almost twenty years.

"'Girl, our love's a winning melody,'" sang Raven's father—also known as Toast.

"'And the beat's coming from my heart,'" crooned Raven's mother—also known as Jelly.

"'We compose a funky symphony,'" Toast continued.

"'And it's going to the top of the charts,'" added Jelly.

"'We've had our share of bumps,'" the two sang together. "'But I'm never, ever down in the dumps. Our love is a smash hit and I know we'll never split—'"

Watching from the couch, Mr. Baxter winced at the word *split*. "Here comes the pain," he warned.

Then it happened.

As Toast and Jelly began dancing to the

song's musical bridge, Toast got carried away. He tried to perform an actual dancer's split, but he ended up tearing some things. His pants for one—and a few tendons in his legs for another.

Paramedics ran in and loaded Mr. Baxter onto a stretcher. His legs were still paralyzed in the split position as they carried him off the stage.

Raven shuddered. "Looks like Toast got burnt."

Cory didn't feel his father's pain. In fact, he had trouble keeping his giggles under control. Then he saw the "payback time" expression on Mr. Baxter's face.

"Should I be running?" Cory squeaked.

"Oh, yeah," said Mr. Baxter, rising from the couch. "Like the wind!"

that's SO raven

Part Two

"It's on!" Raven's father called.

"Ooh, whatever, Jasmine," Raven said. "You're
not the only one in this school who can sing."

"All right, Rae," said Chelsea, "now, this talent scout you saw, what exactly, you know, did he look like?"

"Toast and Jelly...Yes!" Cory cried.

"Honey, you never throw away your memories," Mrs. Baxter said, "no matter how humiliating."

"It is girl *with* bucket!" Raven cried as Jasmine flounced off.

"Man, did you hear that, Rae?" Eddie asked.

The announcer introduced the opening segment:
"Our first tape was sent in by Cory B. I guess he
was too embarrassed to use his last name."

"Okay!" said DJ Eddie T., trying to sound upbeat. "I'm back with my special guest, Raven Baxter."

"Oh, good, a commercial," said Mr. Baxter. "I'm going to go out and get us more popcorn."

"Hey, Eddie," said Chelsea by their lockers the next morning, "everybody loved your show yesterday."

"Hey, there, partner!" Raven cried excitedly. "Look what I got. It's a fan."

"Turn it off! Turn it off!" Eddie yelled over the roar of the fan.

"I had a million great ones and one not-so-great one. Sorry about that, but check this out," Raven said.

Raven's face fell. "Why would I do that?" she asked.

"Help! Help!" Raven and Chelsea hollered.

Chapter One

"**G**ood morning, Bayside!" Eddie Thomas cried from behind the KUDA microphone. He had just started his Monday morning radio broadcast.

In the background, a classic hip-hop tune was winding down. "I'm DJ Eddie T.," he announced, "and that was a little *old school*, going out to the *whole school*."

For the past two weeks, the entire student body had been listening to Eddie's hot new radio show. On Tuesdays and Thursdays he rocked the "hizzle" during lunch period. On Mondays, Wednesdays, and Fridays, he spun CDs first thing in the morning as kids stopped by their lockers and made their way to homeroom.

Eddie had worked really hard to make his new show "the sizzle." But it wasn't easy. The school radio station's studio wasn't exactly state of the art. The room was stuffy and hot, and the tired equipment belonged in the trash. To top it off, his regular engineer was out sick today. But at least Chelsea had volunteered to help out.

"Filling in for Charlie, my engineer who's sick with the flu, is Chelsea Daniels," Eddie told his listeners. He turned in his swivel chair and nodded at his substitute engineer. "Hit my jingle, Chels."

Chelsea seemed a little confused by the studio's wall of buttons, dials, and gauges. In a panic, she pushed a button, hoping that it was the right one. But instead of Eddie's jingle, the next sound they heard was *gobble, gobble, gobble!*

"Hey! I got something!" she declared excitedly.

Yeah, the *wrong* something, thought Eddie, throwing Chelsea a look that said, *Get a grip, girl. Thanksgiving is months away!* He pushed his rolling chair away from the microphone to reach the bank of equipment. Then he hit the correct button himself.

A prerecorded jingle sang out. "*DJ Eddie T. at Bay-side!*"

R-r-i-i-i-i-i-ng!

"We have a caller," announced Eddie, rolling his chair back to the microphone.

"Hey, Mr. DJ," bubbled a familiar voice. "I just love the way you put this whole school-radio thing together!"

Eddie glanced up at the studio's large observation window. He saw a dozen students hangin' in the hallway, watching his show. He wasn't surprised to find Raven standing there with them, waving excitedly—and holding a cell phone to her ear.

Eddie shook his head. "Appreciate the love, *anonymous* caller," he told Raven. "But what can I play for you?"

"You know my jam!" she answered.

"You got it," said Eddie. "Oh, and right after this track, I'm going to be talking to our new foreign exchange student, Vladimir Savelsky."

Eddie flashed a thumbs-up to Vladimir. The supertall student had stepped up to the observation window. He was standing next to Raven and holding up his basketball.

"That's right," Eddie continued. "Vlad's going to lead the Barracudas to our first winning basketball season since . . . well, *ever*."

Eddie spun in his swivel chair. He picked up a broom handle and used it to switch on an old-fashioned reel-to-reel tape player behind him.

Dang, thought Eddie, I have *really* got this

show fine-tuned. He still remembered his very first day on the radio—and all the mistakes he'd made. But since then, he'd figured out ways to cope with the studio's dinosaur-era equipment. The broom handle was just one of many tricks he'd developed.

As the reel-to-reel player rolled, slammin' dance music from a favorite local group filled Bayside's halls. DJ Eddie T. bobbed his head in time with the funky music. Through the observation window, he watched Raven getting jiggy with it, too.

"Ooh, yeah, you better watch out!" Raven cried, throwing her arms this way and that. She jumped back and forth, her legs kicking, her arms waving. "Got to shake my thing!"

As the dance beat started driving, Raven spun like a whirlwind. Without meaning to, she slammed into Vladimir. The string bean basketball star went flying, and so did Raven.

Eddie leaped to his feet, but he couldn't see either of them. Both Raven and Vlad had landed somewhere below the observation window. A few seconds later, Raven popped into view, no worse for wear. She gave Eddie a thumbs-up. Then she turned to the crowd that had formed around them. Everyone looked really upset and worried.

"I'm okay, everybody. I'm okay!" she told the students.

But they didn't care. Every last pair of eyeballs was fixed on the exchange student from Yazablokia. Vlad was Bayside's last great hope to save their losing basketball team. And he was flat on his back and moaning like a sick giraffe.

Horrified, Eddie waited for Vlad to get up again. But it was starting to look like he *couldn't*. The gym teacher rushed over and knelt down. Someone shouted to call 911.

Raven winced at the chaotic scene. "Ooh . . ." she murmured, "my bad, Vlad."

A few minutes later, Raven's favorite dance tune ended. Eddie cued up a prerecorded tape.

"This is for you, Vlad," he announced over the radio. "A little taste of your old country while you wait for the ambulance."

As the national anthem of Yazablokia played throughout the school's public-address speakers, the door to the studio opened. Raven rushed in looking really upset. The crowd in the hallway saw her through the observation window. They began yelling and shaking their fists.

"Hey, hey, hey, people, calm down!" Raven cried defensively. "Dancing accidents happen every day!"

The studio door opened again. This time, the school's Spanish teacher walked in. "Eduardo," she began, "as faculty adviser to the radio station, I am advising you to get a new guest."

"Okay, Señorita Rodriguez," Eddie replied. He thought it over for a few seconds. Then he said, "Well, how about someone loaded with personality who's right here in this room?"

"Oh, Eduardo, please. You're making me blush," said the flattered teacher with a wave of her hand. Then she excitedly turned toward the door. "I'll be right back with my castanets!"

"No, no," Eddie said quickly, "actually, I was talking about Raven."

"Raven?" said the teacher.

"Come on, Eddie," said Chelsea. "Raven can't play castanets."

Raven stared at Eddie. She couldn't believe he was being such a good friend. Any other DJ would be banning me from his studio, she thought. But my boy is trying to give me the chance to make things right with the student body. Eddie's really got my back on this one, Raven realized.

"Well, whatever she plays," warned Señorita Rodriguez, "it better be good."

The teacher left the room, and Eddie motioned for Raven to pull up a chair next to him.

"Okay, here we go, five, four . . ." said Chelsea. She finished the count silently by showing three fingers, then two fingers, and finally pointing to the microphone. Eddie hit a switch and he was back on the air.

"Okay!" said DJ Eddie T., trying to sound upbeat. "I'm back with my special guest, Raven Baxter."

Raven nodded at Eddie and leaned toward the microphone. "Hey, first of all, I'd like to apologize to the student body," she began.

"I'm sorry, basketball team. I'm sorry, citizens of Yazablokia."

"Yeah, it's going to be a tough season this year," said Eddie. "I mean, we were really counting on Vlad to save the team."

"Hey, you know I don't really know that much about basketball," Raven replied, "but I do know a little *somethin', somethin'* about style. Have you seen the uniforms?"

"Of course," Eddie replied. "I mean, I wear one."

"Green and yellow?" said Raven. "That looks great . . . in a *hankie*." She touched her nose and shook her head in disgust.

At the observation window, kids were actually laughing. Señorita Rodriguez was standing at the window too. She noticed how much the kids were enjoying the show and gave Eddie and Raven a thumbs-up.

"So, Rae," Eddie continued, "what you're

saying is if we had better-looking uniforms then we'd win more games?"

"Oh, no, no, no, no," she said. "You'd still stink, you'd just stink in style!"

The kids at the window laughed again. And Chelsea thought this was a great moment to play Eddie's jingle. She hit one of the dozen buttons in front of her.

Yodel-odel-ay-ee-ooooooh!

The audience at the window scratched their heads in confusion. They couldn't figure out what yodeling had to do with the Bayside Barracuda uniforms.

"I'm sorry," Chelsea whispered. "I don't really know what I'm doing."

Raven and Eddie turned to stare their reply. *Well, duh!*

Chapter Two

That evening, Cory and his dad were chilling in the living room, watching television.

"Oh, good, a commercial," said Mr. Baxter. "I'm going to go out and get us more popcorn."

Cory nodded, then frowned when he heard a painful cracking. "What was that?" he asked. The last time he'd heard a sound that scary was in a horror movie, when a skeleton had popped out of a coffin!

"It's just my back," said Mr. Baxter, stretching his large body. "These old bones don't work like they used to."

Cory frowned as Mr. Baxter took the empty popcorn bowl into the kitchen. My dad's talking like he's old or something, he thought. And that's not cool.

"Hey, pardner," boomed a powerful voice. "Feeling old and washed up?"

Cory directed his attention to the TV screen. A big dude in a shiny suit sounded as though he were talking directly to Cory.

"Wasting your life away on the couch with a bowl of popcorn?" said the man in the suit.

Uh-oh, thought Cory, I think this guy's got my dad's number.

"Maybe it's because you're *bald*," said the man on TV.

Whoa, thought Cory, shooting a look to the kitchen door. This dude really does have my dad's number, 'cause he's as bald as a cue ball on a pool table!

"With one of our Gettin' Wiggy With It natural hairpieces, you can be enjoying the life you *used* to have," promised the TV dude.

Cory stared at the images flashing across the TV screen. In a series of quick cuts, the bald Gettin' Wiggy With It guy sported different kinds of wigs. Each wig brought the man into a different exciting adventure.

First, he was wearing a flat-top–style wig and running a football across a field in a big stadium.

"Playing sports," said the Wiggy dude.

Next, he was wearing a long, blond surfer wig. It blew in the wind as he water-skied behind a speedboat.

"Shooting the curl," said the wig man.

Finally, he was grooving to the beat at a rock concert with a brown mullet-style wig on his head.

"Or just plain rocking out," the dude finished.

Suddenly, the Wiggy man was back in his television studio. "What are you waiting for?"

he declared. "Call now and Get Wiggy With It today!"

Finally, the TV spokesman slapped a long, curly wig on his head and did a little old-school rock 'n' roll twist. "Yeah," he said. "Life is good . . . *again.*"

That's it, Cory thought. That's all my dad needs to feel young again! As the Wiggy man's number flashed across the screen, Cory picked up the phone.

"Hey, Eddie," called Chelsea by their lockers the next morning, "everybody *loved* your show yesterday."

"Oh, I know, Chels. It feels good. All that hard work is starting to pay off. Not to toot my own horn, but . . . *toot-toot-toot-toot!*" Eddie smiled and Chelsea laughed.

"*Toot-toot?*" said Raven, walking up to them. "What are y'all *tootin'* about?"

"Oh, nothing much, just talking about my show yesterday," Eddie told her. "Thanks a lot for helping out."

"No problem," said Raven with a smile. She was about to walk away with Chelsea when the Spanish teacher called her name.

"Eddie and Raven!" cried Señorita Rodriguez from down the hall. "Just the people I wanted to see."

Eddie, Raven, and Chelsea all turned to face their Spanish teacher. She beamed at them. "Now, I just wanted to tell you kids how much I enjoyed your radio show yesterday."

"Okay, thanks," said Raven, "but it's Eddie's show. I was just a guest."

"Not anymore," said the teacher with a big grin. "You two had what I like to call 'the chemistry.' You are now *partners*."

Eddie and Raven gave Señorita Rodriguez a disbelieving look, but she appeared to be totally serious. She even sang them their new jingle, for the *Eddie and Raven Show.*

"Wait," said Eddie, still not down with the idea. "You mean you want me and Rae to team up?"

"I didn't sing the jingle for kicks," said the woman. She narrowed her eyes on Eddie. "You have a *problem* with this?"

Eddie gulped. The Spanish teacher was the radio station's faculty adviser. She was the one who'd given him the chance to be on the radio in the first place. And Eddie knew she could take him *off* just as easily.

"No, no, Señorita Rodriguez," said Eddie quickly, forcing himself to smile. "It's cool."

Señorita Rodriguez's frown instantly turned upside down. She nodded her approval. Then she wheeled on her heels and departed.

"The '*Eddie and Raven, Eddie and Raven, Eddie and Raven Show*'," she sang to a group of students as she waltzed down the hall.

Eddie couldn't believe what had just happened. The only thing he could hope for was that Raven would gracefully bow out of this forced partnership and give him his show back.

But Raven didn't see it that way. "Oh, Eddie!" she cried excitedly. "This is going to be so cool. We're going to be partners!"

Chelsea jumped up and down. "Yeah. It's going to be so great, now we can all be together in that stuffy, cramped, overheated little box of a room. It's going to be so much fun!"

Raven and Chelsea rushed off, singing the new *Eddie and Raven Show* jingle. They failed to notice that Eddie's fake smile was hurting more than his face. It was hurting his pride.

"Yeah, so much *fun*," Eddie muttered unhappily as he watched them dance away. The *Eddie and Raven Show*.

*　*　*

Ding-dong!

Mr. Baxter opened the front door that afternoon to find a big man in a shiny suit standing there.

"Excuse me, old-timer," said the man. "I'm looking for Victor Baxter."

"I am Victor Baxter."

The big man looked down at a piece of paper in his hand. "According to my records, Victor Baxter's a much *younger* man."

"I am a much younger man," said Mr. Baxter. "Who *are* you?"

The big man smiled and shook Mr. Baxter's hand. "I'm Cyrus from Gettin' Wiggy With It hair replacements." The man lifted his big display case and strode into the living room. "I got here as soon as I could."

"You got here for what?" asked Mr. Baxter.

"Cyrus!" cried Cory, rushing up to the

cool dude from the television commercial.

"You must be Cory!" cried Cyrus. They shook hands warmly.

Mr. Baxter scratched his bald head. "You know him?" he asked his son.

"I called him," said Cory.

"For what?" asked Mr. Baxter.

Cyrus answered for Cory. "Because every young boy wants a hip, hairy-headed dad." He opened his big display case and pointed inside. Mr. Baxter leaned forward. He saw that the case was filled with assorted hairpieces.

"Oh, come on, Cyrus!" protested Mr. Baxter. "Just because you put a wig on somebody doesn't make them—"

Cyrus slapped a short, natural wig on Mr. Baxter. And Cory held up a mirror.

Mr. Baxter stared at his reflection in awe. He was amazed at the transformation. The wig made him look—and *feel*—ten years younger.

"—a new man," he murmured.

Cory agreed. "Dad, you look so young!"

"Really?" said Mr. Baxter.

Cyrus smiled with satisfaction. He pulled out his order book and pen. "Now, would you be buying or renting?"

Mr. Baxter blinked, not sure yet.

But Cyrus convinced him. "Come on!" he cried, shaking his booty. "Let me see you get Wiggy with it!"

Chapter Three

"I'm going to cool this hot box down," Raven declared the next morning.

Eddie was standing in the middle of the school's small, cramped radio station studio. The *Eddie and Raven Show* was due to start any minute. And Raven was wheeling in some kind of machine on a heavy cart.

"Rae, what are you doing?" Eddie protested.

Raven struggled to position her contribution in the corner of the small studio. "Hey there, partner!" she cried excitedly. "Look what I got. It's a fan. The custodian gave it to me. He said that it used to cool off the whole entire gym before air-conditioning."

Eddie shook his head. The fan looked as big

as a jet engine. And it was probably going to be as loud as one, too. "It's not going to work, Rae," he warned her.

"I bet it still does," she argued.

"Rae, it's *not* going to work—"

But Raven didn't give Eddie a chance to explain. She was so eager to prove herself to him that she simply turned it on.

"Check it out!" she cried.

The steel blades spun like an airplane's turbo props—and they roared almost as loudly. As they produced a powerful wind, stacks of announcements on the studio desk went flying around the room.

"Turn it off! Turn it off!" Eddie yelled over the roar of the fan. "It's not going to work 'cause it's too noisy and blows everything around!

Raven hit the OFF switch, and the noise and wind died down. "Oh, yeah," she said, trying to hide her embarrassment. "I see what you're sayin'. I didn't think about that."

Eddie rolled his eyes. *Great,* he thought bitterly. The *Eddie and Raven Show* is off to a *fantastic* start.

"Hey, team!" Chelsea wore a big grin as she walked into the studio. "Are you guys ready for some radio fun?"

"Oh, yeah, Chels," said Raven. Seeing Chelsea's encouraging smile made her feel better about her first mistake. "You know I'm ready. I've got a million great ideas!"

"Cool," said Chelsea.

"Like the fan?" said Eddie.

Raven didn't miss the nasty tone in Eddie's voice. "Okay," she told him. "I had a million great ones and one *not* so great one. Sorry about that, but check this out."

She walked over to her gym bag and pulled out a large jar. It was filled with multicolored Ping-Pong balls.

"I thought we could do one of those wacky radio contests," said Raven. "You know? Guess how many Ping-Pong balls are in the jar."

Chelsea walked up to the jar and focused on it for a few seconds. "Two hundred and . . . thirty-seven," she guessed.

Raven stared at the girl like she'd just dropped in from planet Freak. "Chels," Raven said very slowly, "how did you know that?"

Chelsea shrugged. "Isn't it obvious?"

Raven glanced at Eddie, and they both took a step away from the girl. Then Eddie shook his head. "Look," he told Raven, "my show was doing fine without all these gimmicks." He headed for the studio door. "I'm going to my locker to get some CDs. I'll be right back."

"Well, hurry back, partner," Raven warned him. "We're on in two minutes."

Eddie stared daggers. "I *know* when we're on."

When the door slammed shut, Raven felt

really stung. She turned to Chelsea. "Whoa, is it me, Chels, or am I detecting a little *attitudinal* problem?"

Chelsea shrugged. Eddie was obviously unhappy about sharing his microphone. "Well, Rae," she said as gently as she could, "you were kind of coming on pretty strong. The show is like Eddie's baby."

"His baby," murmured Raven, thinking it over.

"Yeah," said Chelsea, "and you know, I've never had a baby or anything, but I hear people get really attached to them."

Raven sighed. "Chels, you're right. This is Eddie's baby. He loves it. I don't want Eddie to think I'm taking over. I'm just going to sit back and let him do his thing."

The door opened again, and Eddie was back with a stack of CDs. "Okay, people, it's showtime."

"All right, all right," said Chelsea, checking the wall clock. "Come on, let's make radio magic. Five, four . . ." she counted down. On one, she pointed to Eddie. He hit a switch near the microphone and the ON THE AIR sign above the clock lit up.

"Good morning, Bayside!" Eddie began with enthusiasm. "We're coming at y'all to lift that homeroom gloom. I'm DJ Eddie T.—" He leaned back and gave Raven a nod.

In the chair next to him, Raven slowly leaned forward. "And I'm Rae," she practically whispered into the microphone. "Hey."

As she leaned back again, Eddie frowned. What is up with her, he wondered. Three minutes ago, she was bouncing off the walls. Now, she's got all the spunk of a funeral director.

"So, Rae," said Eddie, keeping his voice strong and upbeat, "why don't you tell the people about your great ideas?"

Raven leaned forward. "Nah," she said into the microphone.

Eddie was starting to get annoyed. "Well, what about the Ping-Pong balls?" he pressed.

"Eh," she replied, then leaned back again.

"Rae," Eddie said firmly, "I could use a little more than 'Eh.'"

Raven bit her lip. She leaned forward again. "Eeehhh."

Eddie threw up his hands. "I don't get it, Rae, I mean, you *said* you had all these *great ideas* and now suddenly you have nothin' to say? You *never* have nothin' to say!"

Raven swallowed uneasily. She was trying to do the right thing here. But it wasn't easy. Maybe the best way to handle this situation was to just be honest.

"Well, Eddie," she said slowly, "this is your show, and I just want to sit back and let you do your thing."

"It's not *my* thing anymore," he pointed out. "It's *our* thing, and you're messing it up, Rae."

Raven's face fell. "Why would I do that?"

"I don't know," said Eddie, thinking it over. "Maybe you want to make me look bad. Maybe you want the show to yourself or something."

"Or, maybe you're trippin'," she snapped. Raven couldn't believe such nasty accusations were coming out of her best friend's mouth.

"Oh, so now I'm trippin'?" said Eddie, his tone hurt and angry at the same time. "I'm not going to stick around and watch you make a fool of me on my own show. I'm out of here!"

As Eddie stormed out, Raven and Chelsea stared after him in disbelief. "Eddie!" called Raven, but he was gone.

For the rest of the school day, Eddie refused to talk to Raven. She knew he was really angry, so she gave him some space to let him cool off.

I'll just wait until I get home, she told herself. But when she tried to call him that afternoon, he hung up on her.

Chelsea couldn't believe that her best friends were fighting. So she volunteered to make things right. Now she was sitting on the Baxters' living room couch with the phone in her hand. And Raven was pacing a groove into her family's area rug.

The beginning of the call went okay. But now Chelsea was just nodding her head and saying "uh-huh, uh-huh, uh-huh."

At last, she hung up the phone.

"Chels, what did he say?" Raven asked worriedly.

Raven's best girlfriend chewed her bottom lip, trying to figure out how to answer with delicacy. "Well," she finally said, "it's really not so much what he said as how loud he was actually *screaming* it."

Raven clenched her fists. "I can't believe that he's still mad at me!"

Chelsea shrugged. "Well, Rae, you know it's Eddie. He's going to get over it."

Yeah, thought Raven, but how long will it take him?

A second later, Raven got her answer. As her entire body tingled with a strange extrasensory energy, her eyes glazed over. Then time itself seemed to stand still.

Through her eye
The vision runs
Flash of future
Here it comes—

Whoa, where am I? Looks like Bayside, but something's different about it. For one thing, a bunch of old gray-haired people are roaming the halls. And there's a weird futuristic sign flashing in 3-D above the gymnasium. It reads—

BAYSIDE 75TH REUNION.

Seventy-five years! **Dang, I've had visions of the future before, but never this far into the future. Oh, whoa, what's that thing? It looks like one of those transporter pads from that starship TV show.**

BZZZZZZZZZT!

Omigosh, that thing is lighting up. I think it actually works! Someone is beaming into the reunion.

Whoa, hold the phone. It's me! I'm so old! I've got snow-white hair and wrinkles like nobody's business. I'm even using a cane. But, dang, I can still dress with style. Just look at that midnight blue silk blouse and slammin' gold-weave necklace!

What's that? The old me is saying something.

"Wow, after seventy-five years, the school still smells the same!"

The transporter pad is lighting up again.

Bzzzzzzzzzt!

Another old classmate is beaming in. It's Chelsea! Her hair is gray, and she's wearing it up in a bun. She's got wrinkles, too.

Old Raven is walking up to her. "Chels, baby, hi," she says. "What took you so long?"

"I'm sorry, Rae," says old Chelsea, "my molecules don't work as fast as they used to."

Old Raven nods her head as if she can totally relate. "Word."

Bzzzzzzzzzt!

Another classmate is beaming in. It's Eddie! He's got wrinkles on his wrinkles. He hasn't lost his hair, but it's mostly gray. He's wearing an oversized plaid shirt, khaki pants, and—omigosh, what is the old man wearing on his feet? White socks and butt-ugly sandals! Fashion disaster!

Old Raven and old Chelsea seem really happy to see him—despite the socks and sandals.

"Eddie!" cries old Chelsea excitedly.

"Eddie. How've you been?" says old Raven with a grin. "Give me a hug."

But old Eddie's not interested in any hugs from old Raven. He pulls away so fast she nearly falls on her wrinkled face!

"How've I been?" snaps old Eddie. "I've been mad."

Old Raven looks devastated. "Eddie! It's been seventy-five years since the radio thing. Let it go."

"Never!" says old Eddie. "I just came here to tell you that I ain't going to never forgive you."

Oh snap! Old Raven is starting to cry. Old

Chelsea is moving to comfort her, and Eddie is slowly shuffling off.

"Eat my dust," he tells old Rae.

"Eddie!" she calls. "Eddie!"

But those ugly, old-man sandals just keep shambling down the Bayside hallway. . . .

When Raven's disturbing vision finally ended, she was trembling. "Chels," she said shakily, "I just saw the future."

Chelsea rolled her eyes. She couldn't see what the big deal was. "Rae, sweetie," she said with a wave of her hand, "you *always* see the future."

Raven grabbed her best friend's shoulders. "Chels . . . it was way, way into the future. Girl, we were at *our* seventy-fifth school reunion."

Chelsea scratched her head. "We went to seventy-five schools?"

Raven smacked her forehead. "Chels! No, it was *our* school."

"Oh!" said Chelsea, finally getting it.

"And Eddie was *still* mad at me," Raven told her.

Chelsea looked dumbstruck. Was this really the end of Raven and Eddie's friendship?

Raven shook her head. "I can *not* let that happen!"

Chapter Four

Mr. Baxter was really into his new hairpiece. He entered the kitchen wearing it, along with the brand-new young-and-hip outfit he'd bought at the Young Urban Planet store earlier in the afternoon. He checked out his reflection in the toaster.

"A new man," he murmured to himself, admiring the hairpiece.

"What's that, Dad?" asked Cory as he strolled into the kitchen.

Mr. Baxter put down the toaster. "Hey, I bet you can't wait to hang out with your new young, hip dad, huh?"

Cory checked out his dad's new outfit. The baggy, denim shorts, oversized denim shirt with corduroy pockets, and high-top boots looked more like something a high school kid—not his father—would wear. But Cory forced a shrug and said, "I'm just happy you're happy."

Mr. Baxter smiled. "Then you're going to get even happier. Check out this funky fresh outfit I got for you!"

He held up an identical outfit to the one he was wearing—only it was Cory's size. "Dad and lad," said Mr. Baxter, handing Cory his new outfit.

"Matching clothes?" said Cory, trying to keep from spewing his afternoon snack. Not even a preschool kid would wear an outfit that matched his parent's. It took dorkiness to a whole new—and *horrifying*—level.

"So go ahead, try them on," said Mr. Baxter. "Then we'll head down to the mall."

"Where people can *see* us?" said Cory, shuddering.

"For shizzle!" said Mr. Baxter.

Cory shook his head. I've created a monster, he thought. "Oh, man."

Later that evening, Cory got to thinking. If my dad's hairpiece were to somehow just *disappear*, then I'd have my old dad back and I wouldn't have to tell him the truth about how I really feel. That's it, he thought. It's time to launch Operation Wig Removal!

With his father sleeping on the couch, Cory tiptoed as close to the snoring man as he dared. Working the jaws of his toy alligator on a stick, he snatched the wig from his father's head. Carefully, he turned and slowly tiptoed toward the front door.

"Hey, where are you going with Daddy's hair?" called Mr. Baxter.

Cory froze and looked back over his shoulder. His dad was sleepily rising from the couch. Okay, *think*, he told himself. "I was just, uh . . . taking it out for some air."

"Cory, grab the wig and come here," said Mr. Baxter, his tone annoyed. "What's going on?"

Cory trudged over. He knew he was busted now. Guess I've got no choice, he decided. Better come clean. "Daddy, your new hair is creeping me out," he confessed, holding out the wig.

Mr. Baxter shook his bald head. "I thought you said that you wanted a younger, hipper dad?"

"Because I thought you missed your hair," Cory explained.

"I have no problems being bald," he informed his son.

Cory threw up his hands. "Then what the heck are we doing?"

Mr. Baxter laughed. "I guess we were just trying to help each other out."

Cory climbed onto the couch next to his father. "Dad," he said, pointing to the matching, father-and-son shirt and shorts, "these outfits don't help anyone."

"Yeah, I guess not," Mr. Baxter agreed.

"I just want my *old* dad back," Cory admitted.

Mr. Baxter smiled and pulled his son into a hug. "You got him."

The next day at school, Raven marched up to her best friend. "Eddie, I've got to talk to you," she demanded firmly.

"Nobody's stopping you, Rae," Eddie spat out, as he rudely kept walking down the hall.

Raven followed, trying hard to keep up. "Eddie, you may not know this about yourself, but you're the type of person who can hold a grudge. I'm talking, like, seventy-five years!"

Eddie stopped and met her eyes. "Look, I

don't hold grudges, Rae," he snapped. "And I'm *never* going to forget you said that."

As Eddie started climbing the school's main staircase, Raven panicked. I am not letting this happen, she vowed to herself. Desperately, she shouted after him. "Eddie, wait! Eddie, I want you to come back to the show!"

Eddie froze. He turned around and came back down to face Raven again.

"Listen, I had a vision—" she started to explain.

Eddie rolled his eyes. "Let me guess," he told her in a dissing tone. "You saw yourself on the radio, falling flat on your face."

For the second time in two days, Raven couldn't believe how low her best friend could go.

"You know what?" she snapped, suddenly more worried about her pride than her friendship. "I take it back. I don't need you. I can do the show by myself. And it'll be a great one. The best show this school ever saw!"

"It's radio," Eddie said flatly.

Raven narrowed her eyes. "Ever *heard*!" she corrected. Then she stormed one way—and Eddie stormed the other.

It was lunch period, time for Eddie's radio show. Raven walked into the studio. She pulled on a pair of headphones and sat down at the microphone.

There, she thought, I'm ready. So how hard was that?

"Hey, hey, hey, it's DJ Rae, on the miz-zike," Raven began, "at *K-U-D-A*. KUDA radio. Yeah!"

Proud of herself for the great beginning, she covered the microphone with her hand and turned to Chelsea. "How was that, Chels?" she whispered.

"Perfect," answered Chelsea. "Very professional. If only we were on the air."

Raven's face fell. "Why weren't we on the air?"

Chelsea shrugged. "I don't really know how to turn on your miz-zike."

"What?!" cried Raven.

"Yeah, that was Eddie's job," Chelsea informed her.

Raven tried not to panic. "Then play some music or something!"

Chelsea threw up her hands. "Again— *Eddie's* job."

"Chels, what was *your* job?" Raven asked in exasperation.

Chelsea shrugged again. "To do whatever Eddie told me."

"Are you serious?" Raven cried. She scanned the wall of equipment. There were dozens of buttons, dials, and gauges. She had no idea what any of them did. "Just great," she muttered.

The clock on the wall was ticking. It was five minutes past the official start time for Eddie's show—and counting.

In desperation, both girls began yelling at each other as they threw switches and pushed buttons. Neither of them saw exactly when the ON THE AIR sign went on.

But it did.

In the school cafeteria, Eddie was just sitting down with his tray of food. Students were eating lunch around him, listening to the start of his radio show. The speakers in the lunchroom crackled, then Raven's voice came blaring out—

"How am I supposed to run this stupid show when I don't know the first stupid thing about any of this stupid radio equipment—"

Chelsea's voice came next. "Rae," she whispered, "we're on the air."

Eddie shook his head in disgust. You wanted it, Rae, he thought. You got it.

"Okay, all right . . . uh . . . let's get to some music," Raven said over the lunchroom's speakers. "I've got stacks of tracks comin' at ya, Ba-a-a-y-s-i-i-i-de."

Back in the studio, Raven looked to Chelsea for some help turning on the music. Chelsea pointed to the reel-to-reel tape machine on the wall behind her.

Raven nodded and reached for it, but it was too far away. She took off her headphones, walked over to the player and reached up to turn it on.

It was way too high and she had to jump to get it going. Frustrated, she jammed the machine's switch up. The reel started spinning, but she'd pushed too hard. The tape started pouring out of the machine and onto the floor.

"Rae, the machine," called Chelsea.

"Bayside, now it's coming at me!" Raven exclaimed in fear, trying to stop the tape from tangling up.

"Ow, ow, ow!" howled Chelsea. She had tried to help Raven by lunging for a prerecorded sound cart. But she'd only made things worse.

"Rae, my hand's stuck!" she cried.

Raven turned to see Chelsea being eaten alive by one of the dinosaur-era sound-cart machines.

"Ow! Ow! Ow!" Chelsea cried again, tugging at the man-eating gadget.

Raven rushed over to help her best girl-friend. But she wasn't sure what to do. "How am I supposed to get you out of here?" she wailed.

"I don't know," Chelsea moaned, "that was Eddie's job!"

Back in the cafeteria, Eddie couldn't believe how badly things were going for Raven. Her radio show was a total disaster.

Señorita Rodriguez walked up to Eddie's table. "Eddie, there you are," she said. "How can you enjoy your lunch when your show is going down the tubes?"

Eddie shook his head. "It's not my show anymore. I'm done with it."

"Really?" said the teacher. "Are you done with that churro?"

Eddie shrugged. So did the Spanish teacher. Then she took his untouched cinnamon pastry and walked away.

"One, two, three," cried Raven and Chelsea together in the radio station studio.

Raven yanked Chelsea out of the cart machine. Together they flew through the air and knocked over the jar of multicolored Ping-Pong balls. They bounced all over the studio.

Desperate to keep the show going, Raven slid back into her chair behind the microphone. "Bayside, Bayside," she said breathlessly. "Okay, how many Ping-Pong balls just hit the floor? Call us now, operators are standing by. Our number is—"

"Is it me, or is it hot in here?" said Chelsea. She walked over to the giant gymnasium fan that Raven had wheeled into the studio the day before.

"Chels, no!" cried Raven.

But it was too late. Chelsea had turned on the giant fan. With a roar like a jet engine, the blades began to spin. Suddenly, Raven felt like Dorothy in *The Wizard of Oz*. The blasting wind sent every loose thing in the studio swirling around her head: papers, Styrofoam cups, Ping-Pong balls, audiotape.

"Chelsea," she screamed, "turn off that fan!"

"I can't," Chelsea shouted back.

"Turn the fan off, Chels!" Raven called again.

Chelsea struggled to step forward against the wind. One step, two steps—then the blasting wind sent her to the floor.

This is messed up, Eddie thought, listening to the shouts of Raven and Chelsea over the noise of the fan.

He glanced around the cafeteria. Everyone was screaming with laugher and pointing at the public-address speakers. His best friends had become total laughingstocks.

But Raven is actually good on the radio, Eddie admitted to himself. Of course, she doesn't have a chance in that old studio with Chelsea.

Oh, *man*, he thought, my best friends really need me. The only question now is—what am I going to do about it?

Chapter Five

"**H**elp! Help!"

Raven and Chelsea hollered for help, but it did no good. The giant fan had kicked up to speed by now. The wind blew the two girls across the room and pinned them against the studio's observation window.

"Whoaaaaaa!" Raven cried.

"Shut it off!" Chelsea yelled.

Raven struggled to pull herself along the desk. She grabbed the microphone. It broke off its short stand, and now Raven was holding onto its wire like a water-skier behind a powerboat.

Finally, she let go, and the fan blew her back against the window again. Now she was back where she'd started, right next to the pinned

Chelsea. Both were being pelted with papers, Ping-Pong balls, and cups.

Omigosh, thought Raven, I am really in trouble here! What are we going to do?!

Knock, knock, knock!

Raven looked up and couldn't believe her eyes. Eddie was standing at the observation window. Her boy was here! He was coming to their rescue!

A few seconds later, Eddie was bursting through the studio door. "Rae, what are you doing!" he began. But as he stepped inside, the blast of the fan struck him, and he was immediately blown against the window with his two best friends.

"Aaaaaaah!" he yelled as his backpack opened and papers flew everywhere.

"Eddie, what do we do?" cried Chelsea.

"Y'all get in front of me!" he told them. "I'll push you toward the plug!"

Eddie braced himself against the wall and pushed Raven out first. As she stood in front of him, she pushed Chelsea out. Then she stretched with all her strength to turn off the fan.

"Pull the plug!" Raven yelled over the roar of the blades.

"Pull the plug, pull the plug!" Eddie agreed.

"Okay!" shouted Chelsea, reaching for the extension cord. "One, two, three."

She did it! Finally the fan's blades stopped turning and all three friends fell to the ground. Raven crawled to the microphone.

"Bayside, Bayside, Bayside," she said breathlessly. "This is DJ Rae. As you can tell, I'm not really a radio person. I'd like to turn it over to DJ Eddie T."

Eddie shook his head, feeling really terrible about how he'd acted. "Rae, you don't have to do that for me."

"No, Eddie, this is your show," she insisted. "You made it what it was."

"Yeah," he said. "But then I couldn't admit that having you here made it even better."

Raven laughed. "Not having you here made it a *disaster*."

"Listen, Rae," said Eddie. "The bottom line is, my pride was hurt and I acted like a jerk. So, if you want to stay on the show and do it with me, that's cool."

Raven smiled, accepting his apology. But she knew this radio stuff wasn't really her thing. "Nah," she told Eddie. "But if you ever need a guest—or a *friend*—I'm there for you."

Over in the school cafeteria, the students had been listening to every word of Raven and Eddie's conversation. When Raven said she'd always be there for Eddie, the kids whooped and clapped.

Eddie thought it was pretty cool himself.

"Thanks, Rae," he said, then turned to Chelsea. "Hit my jingle, Chels."

Dead silence followed for the next few seconds. When Eddie and Raven turned to find out what was going on, they found Chelsea with her hand caught in the wall of equipment again.

"Eddie?" she wailed. "Would ya?"

Eddie sighed and crossed the room to free Chelsea from the clutches of the man-eating sound-cart machine once more.

Dang, he thought, I'm sure glad things are back to normal!

Now that Raven, Eddie, and Chelsea were back to being the three amigos, they agreed to hang together after school.

"Man, this is boring," Eddie complained.

They were sitting on Raven's living room couch, watching Raven's favorite daytime drama.

"The game's on," Eddie declared, checking his watch. He turned to Raven, sitting next to him on the couch, and snatched the remote from her hand.

"Eddie, no." Raven snatched the gadget right back. "You're not turning off my soap. Not until I find out if Tricia's baby is an alien."

Eddie smirked. "Here's a clue, Rae. The kid's got green skin."

"You guys, please stop," said Chelsea. She'd had enough discontent for one week. "You know what can happen when you two start fighting," she warned.

Suddenly, Raven felt her body begin to tingle and the room begin to spin. . . .

**Through her eye
The vision runs
Flash of future
Here it comes—**

Dang, *look at this! I'm back at Bayside's seventy-fifth reunion. Okay? What's up? . . . I see all those old people are still roaming the halls. And there I am. Looks like old Raven and old Chelsea are hanging together again.*

Hey, there's that futuristic transporter pad. And it's lighting up.

Bzzzzzzzzt!

Old Eddie just beamed in. Old Raven and old Chelsea look really happy to see him. "Eddie!" *they exclaim as they shamble up to their old friend.*

Awwww, look! He's giving them a big hug.

"Raven, Chelsea, how long has it been?" *he asks them.*

"Around ten minutes," *says old Raven.* "We left the teleport at the same time."

"I know," *says old Eddie with a warm smile.* "It was just an excuse to hug my best friends."

"Guys!" cried Raven as she snapped out of her vision. "I just checked out the future. We're going to be friends forever!"

"Good," said Eddie, reaching for the remote again. "Then give me the remote. I want to watch the game."

"No way!" cried Raven, holding it away from him. "I want to watch my soap!"

Raven and Eddie continued to argue, their voices rising higher and higher. Chelsea got up off the couch, walked over to the TV, and changed the channel to *her* favorite afternoon show.

"Give me that back!" demanded Raven, not noticing what Chelsea had done.

"No way. It's mine!" countered Eddie.

Chelsea ignored them. She just sat down in front of them on the coffee table and started watching her cartoons.

"Mine!" squealed Raven.

"Mine!" squeaked Eddie.

Cool, thought Chelsea. As long as Raven and Eddie keep arguing, I've got the TV all to myself!

Gaze into the future and take a sneak peek at the next *That's So Raven* story. . . .

Adapted by Alice Alfonsi

Based on the television series, "That's So Raven", created by Michael Poryes and Susan Sherman

Based on the episode written by Michael Carrington

After setting down their bags near the front door, Raven's parents watched their daughter bustin' moves around the living room. They waited for her to stop and talk to them. But she was totally oblivious.

At last, Mrs. Baxter walked up to her daughter. "Raven," she called. "Raven!"

But Raven wasn't listening. Her eyes were closed, and she was still getting jiggy with her all-time favorite jam.

Frustrated, Raven's father walked into the room, seized the remote, and switched off the television. The music stopped, but Raven didn't. She was still getting down with the beat in her head.

Mrs. Baxter cleared her throat, and Raven finally looked up. "Hey, Mom. That's my jam!" she exclaimed, wiggling and shaking. Then she caught her mother's frown. "Uh—and I can stop any time I want," Raven quickly added.

But Rae's booty was still moving. Finally, she reached back and grabbed it. "Stop!" she commanded. At last, all jiggying ceased.

"Raven," Mr. Baxter said in a stern voice, "this is very important."

Raven nodded, all ears.

"We're going away this weekend," he reminded her, "overnight to cousin Brenda's wedding. And we want to feel comfortable that we're leaving the house with somebody responsible."

Raven nodded. She'd heard this before, of course, about a thousand times! "All right!" she replied. "You can trust me."

But her parents didn't look very convinced. They exchanged wary glances before picking up their suitcases and heading for the door.

When Raven saw their expressions, she knew she should reassure them. There was no need to worry. Not with Raven Baxter in the house!

"I promise. You can count on me," she told them, crossing her heart.